I0780649

Where Love Starts:

Go Station

By

Dhatcha

Copyright © 2025

All Rights Reserved

ISBN: 978-1-966642-78-7

Acknowledgment

3

This book is dedicated to my daughter Hanvi Kalav, with love.

And to all those who are better at writing love letters than expressing it in the real world.

About the Author

Dhatcha grew up in a family where stories and tales flowed endlessly. This environment shaped her gift for turning everyday moments into episodes with fairy tale endings in her fictional world. She curates tales inspired by real people who have touched her life, weaving whimsical narratives that reimagine their realities—stitched together on paper into something beautifully new.

Sudden Break

Her kitten heels stand precisely behind the yellow line on the train station platform. It is the usual 7:25 a.m. train, but today, it is delayed by 5 minutes. She taps her left foot in subtle disapproval. Hanica is all about punctuality and consistency. Whether it is the bus or the train, one thing never changes—her book is always with her. As her fresh, blow-dried, crisp, dark brown hair sways gently from her ears to her shoulder, the train slowly arrives. The door opens right in front of Hanica, and as she steps aboard, she spots a corner window seat—rare on a midweek morning. Without a moment's delay, she rushes to open the page where she has plucked the bookmark. The train eases forward.

Her daily journey usually follows the same script—until, just before Toronto Union Station, a sudden, unannounced jolt sends her rocking back and forth, her book slipping from her hands. A fragile reader is startled mid-sentence.

She recovers from a brief moment of embarrassment and adjusts herself, sitting upright with her spine straight and posture composed. Her eyes dart around as she silently prays that no one has noticed the scene.

Luckily, no one has. Most passengers are glued to their phones, some are asleep, and the rest are too absorbed in their worlds to care.

Except for one.

A pair of piercing blue eyes is locked onto her.

Hanica instinctively lowers her gaze, letting her lashes fall to avoid eye contact—but curiosity gets the better of her. She glances back, her warm brown eyes lined with dark eyeliner, meeting his.

He offers a slight, knowing grin.

Hanica responds with a soft smile of her own, then gently lowers her gaze and returns to her book, heart fluttering beneath the pages.

The train pulls into Union Station. Hanica tucks her book into her bag and slips on her sunglasses. She is already in the queue to exit the train and head toward the subway.

The elevator is unusually empty, rare during the morning rush. As she steps toward it, she realizes it has been held open for her by the blue-eyed man.

Surprised, she smiles broadly and says, "Thank you."

The tall, tan-skinned man—around six feet, with striking eyes—returns an inquisitive smile. It is a brief, unassuming gesture, but enough to shift the rhythm of her morning.

The flutter in her chest reminds Hanica of something she hasn't felt in years, since high school, with her first love. That relationship is undone by distance and immaturity.

"Oh, come on, Hani! This is not that," she chides herself as she steps out of the elevator and onto the bustling streets of Toronto.

A graffiti-covered sign reads "F**k you all," held by a ganja-loaded homeless man slumped across the footpath. Hanica tilts her head upward, needing a breath of clarity. Above the noise, the towers stand tall—the Suits building, the Fairmont Union, and other glass-fronted skyscrapers. The hustle and bustle are real in downtown.

Downtown Toronto is alive with energy. Competitive, crowded, chaotic—but also charismatic. It is the city she has dreamed of since high school, ever since watching *Suits* on television. That show has etched an image in her mind of a strong woman working in a corporate role. Now, she is living it.

Toronto has something for everyone: opportunities for hustlers, restaurants for foodies, sights for travelers, and lovers—a place to write charming memories. Life here is busy, beautiful, and precisely the way Hanica has hoped.

By 5:00 p.m., Union Station is buzzing. The crowd surges through the subway platforms. Hanica has just missed her train. She stands on the platform, her kitten heels neatly behind the yellow line, book in hand.

Then, a quiet tug from her instincts:

"Take a peek. Someone's watching you."

She looks up, away from the page.

The same blue-eyed, sun-kissed man—six feet tall, blond—is gazing at her with a smile. She smiles back, then quickly turns to her book.

"Why did I do that? I don't know. Maybe I'm being friendly. Or maybe he is. Is this what telepathy feels like?"

The train arrives. The platform swells with people. Hanica tucks her book into her bag and slips into the train, determined to find a window seat.

This time, she is lucky.

She slides into the window seat.

Across from her sits the man with blue eyes.

The Train Started; The Conversation Started

"I'm Jake, and I love reading, too. Right now, I'm reading Long Walk to Freedom."

Hanica hesitates, "Umm...nice to meet you. I'm Hanica. It's great to hear what you're reading." She smiles at him, her tone warm and inviting. Though she wants to keep the conversation going, her introverted nerves spike, as they often do in moments like this.

Taking a deep breath, she adds, "People call me Hani—like honey."

Wait, what? Why did you say that, Hani? She panics internally. Now he's going to switch seats for sure.

But instead of recoiling, Jake grins from ear to ear. He enjoys the exchange.

Though the train car is tightly packed, Jake and Hanica feel as if they are sitting alone in a lounge, having a one-on-one conversation. The air smells faintly of spiced lattes from Tim Hortons and the soft, woolen scent of autumn coats. It's all in the mind—how we feel shapes how we perceive the world. What feels like chaos to others becomes a time-frozen realm for them. In their space, only comfort and chemistry exist. Silent smiles play on their lips, though no more words are exchanged.

A crackling announcement snaps them back to reality. Their station is near.

Jake's khaki-colored pants rustle as he stands reluctantly. He quickly gathers his only belongings: a brown leather bag with too many compartments.

They both get off at Cooksville.

Hanica has lived in this Toronto suburb for over five years. Jake has been here since college. Yet somehow, fate waits until this exact moment to bring them together.

The right timing takes time. But when it arrives, it moves fast—that's life. Don't question it. Indulge in it. Enjoy every minute. Recognize the version of yourself you become through these serendipitous moments. That's how you live life as an adventure.

Hanica lives in Building 339, just across from the Cooksville GO Station—a 30-minute walk. Jake lives in Building 335, right next door. They are no strangers to these buildings; they've experienced joy, depression, and quiet weekends within their walls. But somehow, time chooses today to reveal this coincidence.

In a world of eight billion people, things happen constantly—but not randomly. Every action, whether positive or negative, causes a ripple that shapes networks and history over time.

So why does this brief meeting spark something in both of them? Do either of you think of it as destiny?

That's up to Jake and Hanica to decide. Every connection requires initiation, and that requires instinct—the courage to pursue what you want.

At home, Zeus—the snowshoe cat—greets Hanica at the door. His dark brown and white fur, icy-blue eyes, and pristine white paws make him look like he's wearing snowy boots. Zeus is Hanica's loyal companion, turning her boring days into cherished memories. He is five and follows her around the home like a shadow.

Later that evening, soaking in a warm bubble bath, Hanica raises her glass of wine and asks aloud, "Why do I feel this way? I barely know him. What if he's already in a relationship? He looks like he should be. Or maybe… he's just good with people. It was just a glance. A smile. A short conversation. That's all. That's all. Don't overthink. Don't overthink."

She takes a deep sip of wine, finishing the glass, and sinks lower into the tub.

Zeus senses danger—or worse, his dinner slipping away—whenever Hanica soaks too long. The poor guy looks like he's planning a rescue mission for his dinner plate.

"Meow…"

Hanica rises and mimics his cry. Zeus, reassured, jumps onto the washbasin and settles in.

Across town, Cocoa—a short-haired British brown cat—is licking the rim of Jake's whisky glass, balanced on the kitchen counter.

"Hey, Cocoa, want some catnip, buddy?" Jake says.

Cocoa's golden eyes widen at the word. Catnip is his equivalent of booze. Jake only gives him a taste when he's in a perfect mood.

A drop of catnip sits on the coffee table. Cocoa pounces on it, rolling happily.

Jake sips his drink and reflects on the encounter with Hanica. A quiet smile crosses his lips. Soon, both man and cat are curled up in bed, fast asleep.

Back in her bedroom, Hanica lies staring at the ceiling, pondering what to wear the next day.

It should be something special. Elegant. Stunning… Pearls. Definitely pearls. Black—that always makes me feel confident. I need to wake up early to blow-dry my hair.

Zeus is already nestled beside her, dreaming of endless treats.

For a heart stirred by love, sleep doesn't come easily.

Eight Minutes Delay

Hanica quickly chooses her lucky autumn boots — not the fastest or most comfortable, but expensive. She misses her usual coffee from the nearby Tim Hortons. Marching to the station at her best speed, she knows she will arrive three minutes late.

The train arrives five minutes early — lucky for all the punctual passengers, but not for Hanica. She sighs and closes her dark brown eyes in a desperate, "Errrr."

A voice behind her breaks the silence: "Missed the train, eh?" Hanica has been expecting to hear that. Jake stands there, hands tucked into his pockets, a brown leather bag slung across his shoulder, smiling warmly.

A sudden rush of happiness hits her all at once. Words tumble in her mind as she gathers herself to respond. Jake's blue eyes catch the soft autumn sunlight, and Hanica's brown hair dances in the warm breeze.

"I'm late. The train was five minutes early," she smiles, just for Jake.

A delay isn't always bad, just like failure in life. Sometimes, these moments steer us toward destiny.

Jake offers, "The next train is in 25 minutes. Want to grab a coffee? There's a shop just by the station."

"Sure, I'd love to," Hanica replies.

They start walking toward the coffee shop — or, as it might turn out, their first coffee date.

"So, Hani, how's your day going?" Jake asks.

"So far, good. I have company, even if I missed the train. How about you?"

"Not bad. I work at Zizzlo downtown as a Senior Data Analyst."

"Zizzlo? That's on Adelaide St. East. I work at DDS Financial Group as a Fund Accountant — two buildings over. I usually hang out at Starbucks on the PATH to Zizzlo."

Jake raises his eyebrows. "Is that so? We've never met before!"

"Glad to meet you now," Hanica smiles.

"Pleasure's mine."

At the coffee shop, Hanica orders a small black coffee, and Jake a small one with milk.

"Downtown's busy. Taylor Swift's concert is today," Jake says.

"The tickets are pricey, and the station will be packed," Hanica notes.

"Expected. Seems most women love Taylor Swift. Who's your favorite?"

"Taylor Swift is great, but I prefer Imagine Dragons."

Jake's eyebrows lift again. "Wow! Imagine Dragons are one of my favorites, too."

They exchange smiles over sips of hot coffee.

Fifteen minutes later, they briskly walk back to the platform.

Hanica stands just behind the yellow safety line. Boarding the train, she searches for a window seat. Jake follows quietly.

"You live near Cooksville Station?"

"Yeah, building 335. Been here over a decade."

"No way! I live in building 339."

"Ohh…ooo!" Jake smiles brightly.

"I like this coincidence."

"Me too, me too," Jake replies, a beat late.

"Wild question — do you have a pet dog?"

"Nope, but I have a cat named Cocoa. Want to see a picture?"

Hanica's mouth drops open. "I have a cat, too! His name's Zeus. I'll show you."

"Wow, another coincidence!" Jake says, proudly showing a photo of Cocoa, a short, brown British Shorthair, with cocoa-colored fur, yellow eyes, and a chubby frame. Cocoa is the talk of the apartment; everyone knows Jake as the muscular guy with the chubby brown cat.

"Aww, Cocoa's adorable!" Hanica's lips pout.

Jake adores her expression — cherry-colored lips, sharp features, eyes framed with eyeliner and mascara, full of stories. He feels like he's talking to a living painting, one he could admire forever.

Still pouting, Hanica shows him a picture of Zeus. "This is Mr. Zeus, my follower."

"He's cute and curious. Not chubby, though. How old?"

"Five years," she says proudly.

"He looks athletic — rare breed?"

"Yes, Zeus is a Snowshoe cat. I adopted him from a rescuer. He loves running around and follows me everywhere in the house."

Hanica then plays a video of Zeus trying to swim in the bathtub.

Jake laughs. "No way, your cat likes water? Cocoa would be petrified if he saw that!"

They laugh together over the adorable cat videos.

"Let me know when you're at Starbucks near my office. We should catch up," Jake says.

"Sure, I'd love to. Can I have your number?"

"Got it. I just sent you a message with my name."

Jake glances at his phone.

"Hi Jake, nice meeting you. This is Hanica."

Hanica's phone buzzes immediately.

"Nice meeting you, Hani."

Second Coffee Date

The clock hits 4:00 p.m. Hanica is already tired of balancing ledgers, so she takes her hands off the system to relax. Her phone vibrates on the desk.

Excitement flutters in her stomach as she checks the notification.

One WhatsApp message from Jake:

"Coffee?"

Hanica replies quickly,

"How about 5 minutes?"

Jake's response is instant:

"See you in 5 at Starbucks."

She rushes to the ladies' restroom, lightly touches up her face with foundation and powder, then traces her lips with cherry-colored liner topped with gloss. Walking briskly back to her desk, she grabs her purse and tells her cubicle mate, "I'll be back in 30 minutes."

Will 30 minutes be enough? What if it runs late? She shrugs off her punctuality worries and heads to the elevator, which opens to Toronto's famous underground PATH.

In harsh winter, the PATH bustles with hot coffee runs and hurried commuters navigating the maze of connected buildings.

Jake messages, "Waiting at the corner table at Starbucks."

Hanica's eyes immediately find him. He waves. She smiles and moves toward the table.

They both order pumpkin spice lattes — the seasonal favorite.

"How's everything with you? All good, eh?" Jake asks.

"I need a vacation!" Hanica sighs.

Jake laughs. "Me too. This routine is stressful."

"Exactly. On weekends, I usually escape to random trails around Ontario," Hanica says.

Jake smiles. "Nice! Do you go alone, or with friends or family?"

Tell him you're single, Hanica's mind whispers wildly. It isn't her fault. She's been single since college, and meeting a kindred spirit makes her consider sides of herself she hasn't explored.

"My family's in Alberta. I moved here four years ago and am building my circle. I usually hike trails alone and explore new restaurants — love trying different cuisines," she admits.

"Ontario's got great food, definitely more variety than Alberta. But the trails don't beat Alberta's — Banff is stunning. I've been three times. My family's here in Ontario. I left home during my college years, so I'm familiar with the area. I can show you some parks, conservation areas, and great restaurants."

Their pumpkin spice lattes arrive.

"Here we go." Hanica sips. "I've never been to Tobermory. Heard it's a must-visit."

"That's true, Hani. We should go before winter. It'll be cold soon, and the Grotto closes — but it's peaceful year-round. Are you free this Saturday?"

Inside, Hanica feels like she's bouncing between earth and sky.

"This weekend? I'm free! I'd love to see Tobermory in every season. But are there rooms available? It's so close."

"Don't worry. A friend owns a lake-facing resort there with great reviews. I'll check with him."

Jake sends her a link with details.

"Wow. The view's breathtaking, both in winter and summer."

"Fish and chips, they are the best. I visit often for the view and the food."

"So, where shall I meet you?"

"We live close. I can pick you up from your apartment."

"Cool. Shall we start early? Maybe 7:00 a.m. Saturday?"

"Sounds perfect."

"I need to load Zeus's food in the auto feeder. He hates that."

Jake chuckles. "Cocoa sleeps next to his feeder like it's his lifeline."

Hanica laughs, relating completely.

"Cool, we have a plan. See you soon."

"See you on the train tomorrow."

They bump fists with soft smiles, a small but meaningful ritual.

Both know the feelings stirring between them, but neither wants to rush. Human manners weave a subtle fabric, letting others judge us gently.

A simple train ride has blossomed into an album of sweet memories. With every conversation, Hanica and Jake grow closer — no longer strangers, but good friends... and maybe something more.

Get Start And Go

You never know which connection will work in your life. A stranger you met yesterday could be your life partner, or soulmate. It reminds us that we thrive as social animals, not solitary workaholics.

The alarm beeps at 5:00 a.m. Hanica wakes, kisses Zeus—who is sleeping on her bed—and springs into her morning routine. She blow-dries her hair, spritzes floral perfume on the tips and curls, applies eyeliner that is neither too thick nor too thin—just perfect—and plumps her lips with light pink gloss.

Her bag is packed the night before, so by 6:45 a.m., she is ready in her apartment lobby.

Jake messages:

"Good morning, starting from my apartment."

At 6:55 a.m., Jake's car pulls up at Hanica's entrance. He jumps out to help with her luggage, then invites her to sit in the passenger seat.

Hanica notices how tidy Jake's car is. Whether at home or work, everything about Jake is clean and uncluttered. She connects his tidiness with clear, clutter-free thinking.

Hanica says, "Your car's spotless. It smells so fresh in here."

Jake smiles. "Thanks. It's always been like this."

"I'm a maximalist," Hanica admits sheepishly. "I have a pouch inside my purse… for my purse."

Jake laughs. "I've seen those TikTok feeds. My uncle's a maximalist, too. He lives in Hamilton in a Victorian house from the late 18th century. He's got at least 500 items in his living room."

Hanica grins. "I'm not there yet."

They share a genuine Duchenne smile.

Jake hands her a small note titled "Itinerary — Tobermory." It has a checklist:

• 8:30 am: Breakfast at Sunset Grill

• 10:30 am: Reach the resort, check in

• 11:00 am: Take a break

- 11:30 am: Walk the Tobermory trail

- 2:00 pm: Lunch

- 4:00 pm: Walk the city

- 7:00 pm: Relax

- 8:00 pm: Best fish and chips

Hanica admires Jake's punctuality, tidiness, and organization. She is none of those things, which makes his traits all the more impressive.

"All set for Tobermory," Jake says.

"This is great. I appreciate your kindness and effort," Hanica says.

"Please, don't be formal," Jake smiles.

"I like the Sunset Grill breakfast," Hanica adds.

Jake nods. "I love their protein-packed platter — my go-to."

"I think we'll reach Sunset Grill in about five minutes," Hanica says.

Jake smiles. "Roads are usually clear Saturday mornings. We might be in Tobermory sooner than expected."

"Hmm," Hanica agrees.

"So, Hanica, what made you relocate?"

"Just the urge to leave Alberta for the financial district of the nation. I'm inspired by the 'Suites' series, which showcases Toronto buildings. The concrete jungle calls me."

"That's good. Good for me, too — meeting you, I mean."

"Same here," Hanica smiles.

They exchange flirty smiles, both aware of the feelings but keeping the tone light. Jake gives Hanica space to get to know him, while she tests his reactions as she shares herself with him.

They arrive at breakfast, and though the ambiance is slow and calm, their conversation crackles like electricity, each exchange drawing them closer.

After a satisfying breakfast, their journey continues.

"You don't eat much?" Jake asks.

"I do intermittent fasting, so I skip breakfast. But I want to keep you company."

Jake laughs. "I have a bad relationship with intermittent fasting. I lift weights and love a carnivore diet."

"I've heard of it. It must help with protein intake. I cook good food, vegetarian and non-vegetarian."

"Wow, you're a good cook? Do you make fish, too? We could even go fishing at Tobermory Lake — have ourselves a barbecue by the water at the resort."

"Seafood's my favorite! We'll need to shop for spices. Let's add that to the itinerary."

"Awesome. Love it."

"Me, too."

Their eyes meet often at traffic signals, always green both ways. Both in their 30s, their playful urges spark in every silence. When they speak, their mature minds keep conversations flowing—never dull, never judgmental, always open.

Arrived at the Destination

After a few hours' drive, they arrive at the resort. Jake has booked two rooms next to each other. Hanica's is the corner room, boasting the best view in the entire resort.

She is beyond content. She knows exactly what she is feeling, her heart pounding with a sudden urge to confess her feelings to Jake. But her inner etiquette guard quickly stops her. You don't know how he feels. What if you scare him off by speaking too soon? Yet, she knows deep down Jake feels the same.

Jake inhales deeply as he lies on his bed, turning his right palm upward as if manifesting the feeling of holding Hanica's hand. In that moment, he imagines a future with her—wife, mother of his children, and more holidays together.

How long will they take to say out loud what time is already weaving between them—a forever kind of bond? Patience may look calm, but it's the hardest virtue when love is no longer a question.

Feeling refreshed, they step out for their walk along the nearby trail.

Hanica gently closes her door, her cheeks slightly flushed. Jake stands just outside his room, waiting, a quiet smile playing on his lips.

A few short minutes apart somehow feel too long, proof of the bond quietly blooming between them.

Jake leads her toward the elevator, and together, they venture down the small path that opens to the trail. The sun is bright, and the breeze carries whispers of Hanica's favorite songs—tunes she can't help but hum along to.

The trees around them blaze in brilliant shades of golden yellow, crimson red, and fiery orange, like nature's own celebration of the moment.

That walk isn't just beautiful—it becomes one of their most unforgettable memories.

"Hanica, I want to know more about you," Jake says.

With rosy cheeks and a shy smile, Hanica replies, "Likewise."

Their conversation flows effortlessly—from memories of their kindergarten teachers to stories from the present day. The world around them fades into stillness, as if time itself has paused. In that space, Jake hears only Hanica's voice, and Hanica, only his.

Before they know it, the five-kilometer walk comes to an end. They've burned calories, yes—but more than that, they've deepened their connection. Hunger tugs at them, but so does something new and undeniable: the awareness that they are no longer just getting to know each other.

They are dating now—both know it, and both want it.

Hanica slips back to her room for a quick break. Minutes later, a soft knock sounds at her door. The scent of her perfume fills the room as she opens it with a smile and a slight nod, inviting Jake in.

His eyes flick to the spread of skincare and body care products laid out on her bed.

"Is this a short trip? Seems like a lot of products to pack," he teases.

Hanica laughs. "Yeah, but buying skincare is my stress buster."

Jake exhales deeply. "If it makes you happy, that's all that matters."

She tosses the products into her tote bag, then presses it into her small suitcase.

"Impressive—you pack that fast," Jake says.

"That's one of my talents," she says with a proud grin.

Jake steps forward and presses a gentle kiss on Hanica's cheek. It is so effortless, so casual, that it catches her completely off guard. For a moment, her thoughts scatter— she can't even remember what she has been saying. Her proud grin softens into a shy, glowing smile.

Jake smiles. "I love the way you smile. You have a beautiful one."

Hanica, still caught in the warmth of the moment, replies softly, "Thank you."

Jake nods toward the door. "Shall we head to the restaurant?"

She walks over to grab her purse and, in a higher, more cheerful voice, responds, "I'm ready—let's go."

As she reaches his side, she gently holds onto his arm, resting her head lightly on his shoulder.

They settle into a cozy booth with a view of the restaurant's softly lit interior.

Hanica feels a bit shy about indulging in a full-course meal. The feeling in her chest is unfamiliar—intense, tender, and quietly thrilling.

"It feels like a dream," she whispers to Jake, eyes glinting with something more than just candlelight.

Jake looks at her eyes softly. "You are my dream, Hanica. I'm living in it right now."

Hanica smiles, heart full. They reach across the table, fingers intertwining in a quiet, affirming touch.

Hanica: "I feel like I'm in an '80s romance novel. Except—it's real."

Jake chuckles at her wit, his eyes never leaving hers.

Just then, the waiter arrives with their meals. As the plates are set down, Hanica leans in slightly, with her soft voice, says, "Bon Appétit to us."

'Dating' is a safe word; 'love' sounds more committed. Hanica and Jake are in love. They both know it, ever since the trail walk.

Jake: "The fish and chips taste yummier now. Try the beer. It's the best in town, it's from a local brewery."

Hanica: "You've got to taste this pasta—it's amazing."

She scoops a bite onto her fork and gently feeds it to him.

Jake accepts it, then takes her hand in his and kisses it softly.

Hanica's heart races. Her thoughts blur into instinct: Put down your food. Kiss him.

She reaches out, cupping his face with one hand while still holding his, and leans in, pressing a gentle kiss to his lips.

Then, in a whisper barely louder than her breath, she says,

"Love you."

Soft words carry the greatest weight—they make or break a relationship.

Hanica's wild instinct melts into the calm strength of her femininity as she whispers. She feels no fear, no hesitation. She knows she wants to initiate this love. Masculinity, after all, quietly longs for bold, authentic femininity.

In that moment, Hanica doesn't question whether it is too soon or whether she should wait for Jake to say it first.

Her love is real, unfiltered, and clear—and that's exactly how Jake likes it.

Jake pauses, eyes drawn to her lips, still tingling with words, "Love you." In that instant, they are the most beautiful lips he has ever adored—because they express what he desires to hear from Hanica.

Jake leans in, kisses her gently and deeply. Then, taking her hand into his, he whispers.

"Hanica, I want you in my life, I love you."

A single tear wells in Hanica's eye, catching the candlelight before it falls. A radiant smile follows, warming her cheeks. She and Jake say nothing, but their eyes speak volumes. Time stands still in that brief moment.

Suddenly, the cozy booth feels too small. Though the food is delicious, their hunger is quenched by love. They feel any physical space between them is a sin. Now it's their turn to express love to each other. Their raw nature is, to speak, neither femininity nor masculinity; it's experiencing singularity through duality.

Jake leans in close, his breath soft against Hanica's ear. "Can we go forward with this?" he whispers.

It's a soft whispering voice. Hanica just expresses her desire through her eyes, and her knees stand up, gently taking Jake's arm in hers.

Soon after paying the bill at the counter, Jake follows Hanica through the elevator. They hold each other tightly. Jake's arm wraps around Hanica's love handle. Hanica takes Jake's arm and quietly rushes to her room.

Back in the room, Hanica opens her door and, with a sudden pull, draws Jake inside, close.

It isn't force—it is certainty. Every person in love feels it: that magnetic boldness when the heart is finally sure.

Jake steps into her world, fully welcomed.

And in the quiet power of that moment, he feels something rare—**pride, trust, and belonging.**

Something every man hopes for, even if he never says it out loud.

Her eyes answer before words can form, and her knees tremble as she takes his arm.

After paying the bill, Jake follows Hanica to the elevator. They hold each other close—Jake's arm around her waist, her hand gripping his.

In her room, Hanica pulls Jake's hand closer with gentle insistence.

It isn't force but desire—the confident pull lovers feel toward one another. Jake feels proud and honored to be drawn so completely into Hanica's world, knowing this closeness is what every man secretly longs for but rarely asks aloud.

Art Of Love Needs No Negotiation

A kiss, deep and lingering, locks Hanica and Jake together on the bed. Their hands work gently, helping each other undress, only to pause again in another tender kiss.

Jake's eyes drink in Hanica's bare form as she closes hers in the embrace. His gaze thanks her heart for welcoming him in, allowing him to discover every part of her. She is like a goddess, her skin glowing golden bronze, reflecting sun rays in a sacred temple.

Hanica feels her feminine beauty blossom under Jake's touch, his fingers tracing delicate patterns, his lips pressing warm kisses on her skin. Confidence and love swell within her. In that sacred space, they are seekers worshipping at the temple of love.

They fall asleep side by side, eyes half-closed yet dreaming with waking hearts, as if they've been lovers for a lifetime. The slow-moving autumn night makes their instincts raw and tender.

Jake shifts toward her, head resting gently on his arms beside her. His fingers find her navel, tracing softly. He slouches closer, laying his head against her chest. Her nipple senses his hot breath and hardens in response.

The comforter beneath them bears witness to their journey—from shy touches to bold embraces, from tender warmth to burning desire. It seems almost too much for one night.

"Hani, I love you. Your mind, your voice, everything about you is exactly what I imagine. I love your body, and I want you in my life," Jake says, holding her right hand firmly.

His clear blue eyes shine with devotion. She knows then that this man is hers—the way she has always wanted to feel.

"Jake, I love you," she whispers, pressing her hand into his.

He leans in, kissing her deeply this time — a kiss heavy with trust and confidence.

"Hani, we should start having a family." Jake smiles gently.

"I love kids, too. I want at least three." Laughs Hanica softly.

"Haaaa… you'll have to give us at least a year, I'm no Superman — definitely not my sperm."

Hanica puckers and smooches him playfully.

They know they are different in many ways, but they love those differences and don't want to negotiate them away. Marriage might require some agreements under one roof, but their love embraces the contrasts.

They are ready to take the next step: meeting each other's families.

"Two weeks from now, my parents are visiting for a small get-together. I want you to meet them," Hanica says.

"Perfect. I'd love that," Jake replies with quiet certainty.

"Hani, I text my mom about you this morning. She's excited for us and wants to talk on the phone."

"I'd be happy to," Hanica says warmly.

Family Time

Jake calls his mom on WhatsApp.

"Mom, I have Hani with me. Would you like to speak to her?"

Maria's voice comes through, bright and excited. "Sure!"

Hanica smiles into the phone. "Hi Maria, how are you?"

"Oh, Hani darling, I'm good! Thank you. How are you?"

"Doing well so far."

Maria chuckles. "Jay's told me all about you."

Jake adds quietly, "Mom, we've decided to meet the families."

Maria beams. "Ken, it's Jay — and it's positive!"

Jake whispers to Hanica, "I told them I'm interested in you and that I'll probably bring you to meet them soon. They're really excited."

Hanica smiles. Jake's family feels warm and welcoming already.

Suddenly, Ken's voice comes on the line. "Jay, give the phone to Hanica. I'm Ken, Jake's dad. Thank you for accepting my son and giving him a dating life."

Hanica laughs aloud. "Hello, Ken. It's nice to speak with you. I look forward to meeting you all."

Ken chuckles warmly. "You're most welcome anytime, sweetheart."

A sweet voice interrupts. "Who are you talking to, Daddy?"

Jake smiles. "Oh, that's my little sister, Jenni. She's adorable. I told her you look like her Barbie."

Hanica grins. "Hi Jenni, this is Hanica. I'm dating your big brother."

Jenni's voice is curious. "Okay... are you the Barbie?"

Hanica giggles. "Yes, I think so."

Jenni squeals. "I want to see you!"

"Sure, sweetheart. I'd love to meet you, too. Let's see each other soon."

"Bye!"

Jake says, "Jenni, sweetie, bye now. Give the phone to Papa."

Ken returns. "Okay, son, we won't keep you. Have fun, and let's plan our meetup soon. Hanica, take care. See you soon."

Maria chimes in warmly, "See you soon, guys. Love you, Hani."

"Love you all, Maria, Ken, and Jenni. Take care. Bye!"

Jake sighs happily. "That was brief but good. Jenni's ten — a real miracle baby."

Hanica smiles, touched by the love in his family. "You have a wonderful family. They seem so sweet."

Jake nods. "They really are. It's the family I want to build."

"So, we're meeting your parents two weeks from now, right?"

"Yeah, they're coming to see the University of Toronto campus. My brother Harry got an offer for his undergrad there."

Jake teases, "Cool. Make sure he brings his broomstick along."

Hanica laughs uncontrollably. She and Harry always fight over silly things growing up — a constant source of amusement for their mom, Hera.

"My mom is Hera, and my brother is Harry. You know him now. My dad is Hanish. All our names start with H."

Jake raises an eyebrow. "Do we have to name our kids starting with H, too?"

Hanica grins. "I have that doubt too." She pulls up a family photo on her phone.

The picture is taken at Moraine Lake in Banff National Park.

Jake zooms in on her dad's face. "You look just like your dad—if he wore a wig, eyelashes, and lipstick," he jokes.

Hanica laughs. "In my culture, if a girl looks like her dad, she's lucky."

Jake smiles. "You're lucky to have me."

"I know," she teases.

"Just make sure your dad doesn't grow long hair," Jake adds playfully.

"That's enough for today, Jay," Hanica smiles brightly.

Jake kisses her lips. "Let's start again. Allow me to discover more."

She grins mischievously. "It's my turn, Jay. Relax and enjoy our company."

Meet Family H

Hanica feels safe and secure whenever she is with Jake. She wants confidence in the relationship, and Jake does too. Their drive back to her apartment is filled with talk about their families—the ones they have and the ones they dream of building together.

Love is real. It doesn't need matching interests; it's the spark that makes people dream big and risk everything for each other. For Hanica and Jake, love is that dream come true, embodied in the partner they have always imagined. Jake knows it's love at first sight but keeps it to himself. For Hanica, it's Jake's simple, clean way of living—no drama, just honesty—that draws her in. They are true to themselves and each other, and that makes their bond strong and special.

The day arrives. Jake knocks on Hanica's apartment door, flowers and chocolate in hand.

The door swings open, revealing a 5-foot-7 young man with round spectacles and a broomstick in one hand.

Jake smiles. "Harry, her brother, a nice cosplay buddy."

Harry grins and slaps Jake's hand in a high five.

"Thanks, buddy!"

"Congrats on being selected for the University of Toronto," Jake says.

"Thanks, and congrats to you both!"

Hanica's father approaches, a tall 6-footer with warm, tanned skin.

"Hanish," he says, shaking Jake's hand firmly.

"Hello, Jake, lucky guy. Hanica's told us so much about you. We're happy to meet you. How are you?"

"Thanks, Hanish. I'm doing well. Lucky to have your daughter," Jake replies politely.

Hanica watches the scene with moist eyes and a bright smile. Hanish catches her gaze and sees the pride and comfort shining through—proof that eyes never lie.

"Hello Jake, I'm Hera, Hanica's mom. We're so glad you're here. Please make yourself comfortable. Hanica mentioned you like fish and chips—I made a South Asian fish fry. Hope you like it."

"Oh, thank you! Please accept these flowers," Jake says, handing them over.

Hera smiles warmly at Hanica's glowing face. Her baby girl has found her sweetheart and seeks their approval. Hera is proud—Hanica has never been this happy before.

Jake feels the close-knit family vibe immediately and thinks about introducing them to his family.

"So, Hanish, how do you like Ontario?" Jake asks.

"It's good—weather's bearable and safe. I worked in Toronto back in the early '80s. Met Hera at a bar near the CN Tower, and we got married in three months."

"Cool! When did you move to Banff?"

"That wasn't planned. We booked a 15-day honeymoon in Banff and fell in love. Hera then became pregnant with Hanica, and we decided to settle here. Hanica basically gave us our ticket to Banff."

Jake looks at Hanica, impressed.

"Wow."

"Shall we have dinner?" Hanica suggests.

"Yes, everyone's starving," Harry chimes in.

Laughter fills the room. Jake has never felt this comfortable with any family except his own. It's the first time he feels his love and comfort can extend to his partner's family, too.

At the end of the get-together, Hanish looks at Jake the same way he looks at his son Harry—warm, approving eyes. Jake notices the silent exchange; Hanica communicates with just a look and a smile, and her father does the same.

"Next week, I'm taking Hanica to meet my parents," Jake says. "They live in Brantford, just a few miles from Cooksville."

"I'm excited to meet them and your little sister," Hanica replies.

"Please send our warm regards," Hera says kindly.

"Absolutely," Hanish adds. "We'll be here the next three weeks."

"Sounds like a plan," Jake smiles.

The evening goes smoothly. Love has woven strangers and their families into one.

As Jake kisses Hanica goodbye in front of her parents, Harry watches with amusement. He catches both kisses and sees his sister blush shyly. After Jake leaves, Harry reenacts Hanica's shyness for their parents' amusement, making her laugh until tears come. She hasn't even realized how shy she looks—until her brother shows her the fun side of it.

Jake's Family Welcomes

It is the tail end of autumn in Ontario, with the first snowfall expected soon. Months have passed since Hanica and Jake began dating. Time seems to fly. Every weekday, they travel together to Toronto, and weekends are spent cozied up in either of their apartments. They love each other's company and are planning to move in under the same roof.

Jake drives Hanica to Brantford, sharing colorful stories of his childhood in his hometown. The two-hour journey feels like just a few minutes. When they arrive, Maria and Ken stand on the front porch, waving as Jake's car pulls up.

Hanica greets them with gentle hugs. She hands Maria a basket filled with cookies and freshly baked focaccia.

Hanica: "It's so nice to meet you both, Maria and Ken."

Ken: "Don't be formal—we're just glad to meet you both! Come on in. Hey Jay, she looks beautiful. You're a lucky guy."

Maria: "Absolutely, Jay, she's stunning."

Jake smiles. "Hani, my mom's a fantastic cook."

Ken laughs. "That's why I haven't had a proper BMI over 4 decades!"

The family chuckles as they step inside.

Jake's family home is a beautifully maintained Victorian house built in the late 18th century. The interior is rich with character—antique furniture lovingly restored and still in daily use. Hanica recalls when Jake said, "My mom and dad are always busy maintaining the house and ranch"—he isn't joking.

Jennifer, known as Jennie, hugs Jake from behind. Jake smiles and introduces her to Hanica.

Hanica hands Jennie a girly gift she has thoughtfully brought.

Hanica: "Here, sweetheart, you look adorable."

Jennie grins. "Thanks, Han. I'll show you my Barbie collection sometime."

Ken: "Not now, Jennie. It's brunch time."

Maria: "Jay, help Hani feel at home here."

Jake: "Of course, Hani, I'm at your service."

The family shares a long, laughter-filled brunch around the dining table. Delicious food, warm stories, and easy conversations flow freely. Jake's family is fun-loving and harmonious, and they welcome Hanica like the daughter they never had.

After brunch, Jake gives Hanica a personal tour of the house, sharing the stories behind each treasured piece. She knows she isn't just walking through a home—she is stepping into his childhood and memories. She loves being there with him. A woman enters not just a man's house, but his heart—and it is clear Jake's heart is hers.

When they reach his room—a cozy space with intricate wallpaper, a nineteenth-century canopy bed, and a late eighteenth-century study desk—Jake gently takes Hanica's chin and kisses her softly. Hanica wraps her arms around him and falls onto the bed.

Jake: "Hani, I want to be your husband. Will you be my life partner?"

From his shirt pocket, Jake produces a simple gold ring and slips it onto her finger. Tears swell in Hanica's eyes as she accepts it.

Hanica: "Jake, I love you. Let's start a family."

Their tears witness the proposal; words are no longer needed. Kisses and embraces speak the language of their love.

The ring Jake gives her has special meaning—it is the one his parents gifted him when he turned twenty, crafted from his late grandmother's wedding ring and resized to fit Hanica's finger. He has ordered a matching ring with her name engraved for himself.

Hanica helps Jake wear his ring. They stay close on the bed, Hanica resting her head on his chest with her eyes closed.

Near the window, a red cardinal perches on a branch.

Hanica opens her eyes to the peaceful, magical view.

Hanica (whispering): "Jake, look—a red cardinal."

Jake, half awake, smiles. "It's nest is in that magnolia tree. It's about 100 years old. The blooms look like lotus flowers on the branches."

Hanica: "Wow, magnolias are my favorite. My parents planted one in our backyard when I was six."

Jake: "Wait until next spring when it blooms. You'll love this place even more."

Hanica: "Jake, can you take me to see that tree?"

Jake kisses her softly. "Sure, my sweet magnolia."

Garden Where Love Blooms

Jake's backyard is majestic. Two huge willow trees and three magnolia trees, each nearly a century old, stand proudly. The highlight of the garden is the rose bushes—thick, woody, and blooming in various colors, their branches climbing the walls and even the roof. These rose shrubs were planted in the late eighteenth century and have been lovingly maintained ever since.

Jake smiles at Hanica. "I've witnessed all the seasons in this garden since I was a kid. But today is special because this garden is looking at you as its owner. Honestly, I should have proposed to you here."

Hanica returns his smile. "Jake, I'm happy wherever you propose."

Her eyes catch sight of a small bench nestled beneath one of the willow trees.
"Can we sit on that bench?" she asks.

"Sure, but be careful—the dry leaves pile up near the pond, and you won't see it until you're close," Jake warns gently.

He leads her to the bench. They sit quietly for hours, discussing plans for their wedding.

Marriage is a big step, one that needs careful thought and execution.

Hanica speaks softly, "If it's going to be a small gathering, why not have it here, in your garden? Next spring would be perfect."

Jake raises an eyebrow, surprised by her charm. "You're so simple, Hanica. You don't know how attractive that makes you." He holds her hips tenderly.

"I don't want an extravagant wedding," she replies. "I've always dreamed of something intimate—less drama, more joy. I love flowers—magnolias and roses, especially. Your backyard is beautiful, and it even has a pathway like a wedding hall. Let's have our wedding here."

Jake smiles warmly. "As you wish, Hani. I'll tell my mom and dad—they'll be thrilled. Mom's always said this garden could hold a wedding crowd. Let's surprise them."

Suddenly, Jennie rushes over to the bench.

"Shall we play? Barbie's parade is waiting!" she exclaims.

Hanica laughs. "Jennie, sweetie, we were just talking about walking in this garden as bride and groom. You should have your Barbie parade at our wedding."

"Can I be your flower girl?" Jennie asks eagerly.

"Of course! You'll be our flower girl, dressed like a princess, with braided flowers in your hair and a tiara," Hanica promises.

Jennie is so excited she runs back into the house, shouting, "They're getting married here! I'm the flower girl!"

Maria and Ken hear Jennie's joyful voice and smile. Maria's eyes glisten with happy tears.

Ken kisses Maria's cheek. "Here we go, another beautiful chapter in our lives, just like we hoped."

"I'm thrilled, Ken," Maria whispers.

"Me too, honey. Let's make sure we support whatever they decide without pressuring them."

Maria takes a deep breath. "Okay, okay... this is too exciting!"

Jake speaks up, "Mom, Dad, we're moving to the next phase—we're getting married in the garden next spring."

Maria and Ken embrace, overwhelmed with joy.

Maria's excitement bubbles over. "Marriage in our garden... wow! I need to plan this right away. I'll call the lawn service. Spring is when more than a hundred tulips bloom here—it's magical. The gardener will prune the roses and bushes, too. We don't have much time, but leave it to me. Pinterest will envy our garden wedding!"

Ken laughs. "Oh no, your mom's Pinterest mode is on! Maria, I'm at your service."

Laughter fills the house, carrying the family's happiness.

Hanica smiles warmly. "Maria, Ken, my family is here in Ontario. They'd love to meet you next week."

Maria nods eagerly. "We'd be delighted to have them. There's so much for our families to talk about. I'm so excited for you both—love you."

Hand in hand, Hanica and Jake leave the house and head back to Jake's apartment, hearts full of hope and joy.

62

Two Families, One Mission

The following weekend, Hanica's parents drive to Brantford to visit Jake's home. They travel in a separate car, while Hanica and Jake have already arrived the night before. Hanica sits in the living room, flipping through Maria's book of rose photographs, waiting for her family.

Maria and Hanica have become best friends after their first meeting. They share a love for baking, a taste for classic decor, and a mutual obsession with flowers. Hanica even admires Maria's sense of style and design more than her own. Maria has already prepared a detailed list of floral arrangements, wedding color themes, and menu options for Hanica to review and adjust. The previous evening is spent visualizing their dream wedding, with Jake offering his occasional input and cheerful nods of approval.

As Hanica chooses roses for her bouquet, the sound of a car engine draws her attention. Her parents have arrived. She jumps up from her seat and hurries toward the front door, only to find that Ken and Jake have already stepped outside and warmly welcomed them in.

Ken, beaming with pride, gestures to Hanica. "This is our daughter-in-law. And my Jake is lucky to have found her."

Hanish and Hera exchange smiles with Ken. "Hello, Mrs. Jake," Hanish greets playfully.

Maria steps forward, her arms open. "Welcome, family H. Please come in. This is our humble wedding venue."

Hera embraces Maria tightly. "Hanica's told us so much about you. Thank you for the love and care you've shown her. She's truly fortunate to have found not just Jake, but your whole family." Her eyes glisten with emotion because, to a mother, seeing her daughter loved and accepted is one of life's greatest joys.

What follows is not a first-time meeting—it feels more like a reunion.

Ken, Hanish, and Jake quickly form one circle; Hera, Maria, and Hanica naturally form another. Meanwhile, Harry and Jennie—caught somewhere between kids and young adults—are left to navigate their own sibling roles in the wedding.

The women take over the formal dining lounge, while the men claim the bar counter near the kitchen. The house buzzes with laughter, conversation, and wedding ideas. Plans for shopping trips are made, invitation designs discussed, and the layout of the bride's walk through the garden is hotly debated.

Jennie twirls around the room excitedly. "I'm going to wear a pink gown with pink roses and pink shoes!"

Ken chuckles. "Done, sweetheart. We just need to pick the date now."

Jake speaks up. "The second month of spring would be perfect—plenty of time for the lawn and flowers to bloom."

Maria agrees. "We're ordering extra floral decorations too, so we're covered."

"Mid-April?" Hera suggests.

"Maybe the last week of April?" Hanica counters thoughtfully.

Jennie gasps. "That's my birthday! April 30th!"

Hanish smiles. "Then we'll have a separate cake just for you."

Jake looks at Hanica. "What do you think—April 30th?"

Hanica nods with a warm smile. "It sounds perfect. That gives us four months."

Ken chimes in, "Plenty of time to plan everything just right."

The room fills with cheerful energy as each family member takes on their role in the step-by-step planning process. Hanica and Jake share a quiet glance amid the buzz. There is something serene and deeply fulfilling about that moment—two families coming together for one mission: their love.

For souls that truly desire each other, only silence can create distance, not time. Though they have met just months earlier, Jake and Hanica already see themselves growing old together. That quiet confidence in their bond is what makes everything feel so natural—and so right.

Christmas Gift

Every year, Christmas brings joy—family gatherings, laughter, gifts, and comforting food. But this year is unlike any other. The family has grown, and so has the love. Gifts feel more meaningful, and every shared moment carries a new sparkle.

Hanica and Jake, accompanied by both their families, visit their trusted goldsmith's shop to place the final order for the wedding jewelry and a custom ring case. Hanica chooses all pieces in gold—simple, timeless, and elegant, without a single diamond. It reflects her classic taste, and Jake follows her lead with admiration. To him, everything she chooses carries meaning beyond aesthetics—it is her personality cast in metal.

Back at Jake's house, the couple retreat to his room for a quick refresh. Jake wraps his arms around Hanica and whispers, "You look even more attractive today. The ornaments you tried on—so elegant, so you. Honestly, you look irresistible."

Hanica smiles and smooths his collar. "That's because I have you by my side forever now," she replies, kissing his nose with playful affection.

At the dinner table, Hanish's chicken curry is the undeniable showstopper. Jake's family isn't accustomed to bold spices, but Hanica's family thrives on flavor. Her cooking has already won Jake over—each dish is simple, yet infused with spices that transform it into something magical.

On that Christmas night, the final wedding menu is set. It leans heavily toward spicy, flavorful dishes—an adventurous choice for Jake's family. But Ken, now a devoted fan of hot sauce thanks to Hanica, pushes for it proudly. That boldness will soon be reflected in the marriage itself—vibrant, full of surprises, and delightfully unforgettable.

Plans for the guest list are postponed until after New Year's Eve. Jake and Hanica agree to keep the celebration intimate—fewer than fifty guests, just close family and friends. The garden can accommodate more, but they want every face to matter. Roses and tulips will dominate the landscape, and at Hera's request, lavender wisteria will drape the trellis where Jake and Hanica will exchange rings and vow their forever.

Later that evening, as Hanica helps Maria load the dishwasher, Maria glances at her warmly.

"Before New Year's, I'd love for you to meet Jake's Aunt Mary. She'll be thrilled to see you."

"I'd love that," Hanica replies. "Jake told me she was a big part of his childhood."

Maria nods, eyes softening. "Mary is one of the kindest souls I know. She chose not to remarry after her husband passed in the nineties. She raised Jake like her own and now dotes on Jennie. One day," she adds with a wink, "she'll be spoiling your little one, too."

Hanica smiles, heart full.

Christmas night comes to a gentle close. Jake's family hosts the evening with grace, and the next morning, Hanica's family leaves for Banff. Harry, now officially accepted into the University of Toronto, returns to campus with their parents.

Hanica and Jake stay behind, soaking in the quiet joy of the holidays. New Year's is just days away.

"Hanica," Jake says as they pack, "shall we head to my aunt's place? She wants us to stay a couple of nights."

"Sure," she replies. "Is it far?"

"Just a two-hour drive," Jake says. "Pack for three days. Aunt Mary insists."

"No problem," Hanica smiles. "I'll pack a few of your sleepwear things too."

Jake leans in, "You're the best, Hani. I'll go fill up the tank—be ready when I'm back."

"I'm almost done packing," she calls after him.

Maria appears at the doorway with a gentle smile. "Hani, come have some tea with me while you wait."

Hanica nods warmly, "On my way!"

J & H Are Counting Down the Days Together

The day after Christmas, with Hanica's family on their way back to Banff, Jake and Hanica pack up and head to his Aunt Mary's ranch. Though snow falls heavily, blanketing the roads and trees in white silence, nothing can stop them from reaching her.

Nestled in the middle of a snow-dusted ranch stands a stunning Victorian home. The snow reflects sunlight so brightly it blurs their vision, but on the front porch stands a woman whose presence glows warmer than the house itself.

"Aunty!" Jake says, running up to give her a tight, warm hug.

"Love you, Jake," Mary replies, her eyes sparkling as she turns to Hanica. "And I see you've gotten lucky in life."

"Hi, Aunty Mary. So nice to meet you," Hanica says, returning her kind smile.

Mary reaches out and hands her a small gift box. "Open it, Hani."

Inside is a delicate gold pendant with the engraving

"J & H"

Jake leans closer for a look. "Aunty! That's so thoughtful. Hani's been looking for something like this. You two have the same taste."

Mary laughs. "Maria said the same. I'm glad you like it."

Jake opens the bright red front door, adorned with an ornate lion-head knocker, and Hanica freezes for a moment. Inside, the house is a scene from a Gothic novel—tall stained-glass windows spill colored light across the velvet furniture, heavy brocade drapes sway gently at the edges, and every detail feels like a portal to another world.

"She writes science fiction," Jake whispers. "And in every book, her villain is named after her late husband. But don't be fooled—she has the kindest heart."

Mary reappears with a tray of tea. "Hani, black tea or milk tea?"

"Always black," Hanica replies.

"Perfect. Same here," Mary grins. "Jake, go settle your bags in the room I prepared upstairs. Hanica, come on. Let's have some 'us' time."

"Can you show me around first? Your home is incredible," Hanica says.

Mary's eyes twinkle. "Of course. Victor—my late husband—was obsessed with the Gothic style. Black was his favorite color. After he passed, I slowly turned this place into a tribute to his memory. It brought me peace."

She leads Hanica to the kitchen—a bold blend of black and red like something from the Addams Family. "Jake learned to bake right here," she says proudly.

"He's great at baking," Hanica smiles. "So am I."

Mary squeezes her hand and leads her to the kitchen island, where an array of treats awaits. Cookies, pastries, and a two-tier cake are decorated with the initials J&H.

"How do you like your wedding cake?" Mary asks. "These are samples from a friend of mine. I thought you should try before you decide."

Hanica is overwhelmed. Jake has told her about his aunt's legendary planning skills, but seeing it firsthand leaves her speechless.

"Mary, this is so much. I don't know how to thank you."

Jake wanders in and takes a bite. "This cake is incredible. And the pasta? Wow."

Mary claps her hands. "Perfect! The couple approves. Now for the next surprise—Hani, tell me, do you know what style you want for your wedding dress?"

Hanica laughs. "Not really."

Jake teases, "She'll probably wear jeans and a T-shirt."

Mary gives him a look. "He would love you in anything. But come with me, Hani."

She leads Hanica up to the attic and opens an old chest. Inside lies a breathtaking silk wedding gown with intricate pearl detailing.

Hanica gasps. "Is this yours? It's stunning! The pearls— oh, wow."

"I wore it at my wedding. It even made the local magazine for its craftsmanship. If you wish, it's yours."

Hanica hesitates. "Are you sure?"

"I'd be honored. Come, let's try it on. Close your eyes and trust me."

Mary is a skilled tailor, among many things. After Victor passed, she taught herself a new skill each year—sewing, coding, gardening—anything that makes her feel alive again. She adjusts the corset with practiced hands, smoothing the dress to fit Hanica's frame.

"Okay, open your eyes."

Hanica turns to the mirror and gasps. Her reflection takes her breath away—not just because of the dress, but because she finally sees herself as a bride.

Tears well in her eyes as she turns to hug Mary. "This is... perfect. Thank you. I never imagined my wedding dress would be this special."

Mary smiles softly. "I knew it was meant for you. Now, shall we surprise Jake?"

She calls out with a wink, "Jake! Can you bring a hammer up here? Some nails need fixing!"

Jake comes bounding up the stairs. "Alright, what needs—wwwoooooow."

His jaw drops as he sees Hanica.

"You... you look—" he stammers, walking slowly toward her. "I never imagined... You look absolutely stunning."

He kisses her gently on the cheek. "You'll be the most beautiful bride I've ever seen."

Mary stands in the doorway, watching them. In that moment, her heart swells with joy. She has spent years building a quiet life after loss, but now, watching Jake and Hanica begin theirs, she feels something new: Peace.

Happy Marriage Bloomed in the Garden of Love

Winter melts away swiftly, and spring blossoms, ushering in the long-awaited wedding bells and carefully laid preparations. Everyone in the family is busy—except Jake and Hanica. The couple is left to dream, to soak in the calm before the celebration, knowing they stand at the threshold of a lifetime together.

Maria and Ken's home transforms into a garden fairytale. The backyard overflows with colorful floral arrangements—roses, magnolias, tulips. Crystal chandeliers sway under the wedding tent. A white dance floor shimmers beside the pond, and elegant ceremony chairs line the aisle. A warm, handcrafted wedding sign greets guests at the gate and porch, welcoming them into the most important day of Jake and Hanica's lives.

Jennie walks the aisle first, scattering rose petals with calm focus. She wears her perfect pink gown, just like her Barbie doll nestled in her flower basket. Graceful and poised, she is every bit the flower girl her family has dreamed of. Maria and Ken watch her with pride swelling in their hearts.

Then, the music swells. The moment has come.

Hanish walks Hanica down the aisle.

She wears a majestic gown of silk and pearls, a flowing veil cascading from her hair. Her face, though partly hidden, radiates quiet grace and overwhelming joy. Hanish and Hera beam with pride and love—this is their little girl, now a bride, stepping into her new beginning.

As Hanish reaches the altar, he gently places Hanica's slender hand into Jake's.

Jake slowly lifts her veil.

And there she is. Beautiful. Ethereal. His Hanica.

He falls in love with her all over again.

A good marriage is when you fall in love with the same person again and again, at every chapter, through every change.

For Hanica, it feels like their worlds have collided and fused. There is no longer a Jake and a Hanica. Only them. One. Whole.

The world stands still.

Rings are exchanged. Vows whispered like poetry. A kiss seals it all.

And then, Jake lifts his bride in his arms as Hanica tosses her bouquet into the spring air, a symbol of her joy taking flight.

Cheers erupt, laughter spills over, and the music swells once more.

The dance floor fills with family and friends, their steps weaving memories into the fabric of that evening. Generations of love, stories, laughter, and happy tears converge on that garden floor.

The sky turns a dreamy hue, clouds tinged with soft pink, like the blushing petals all around them.

Under that sky, surrounded by love, a new chapter blooms in the garden where it all began.

Go Station

A few years later, Jake and Hanica hurry down the familiar platform, hand in hand, after dropping their 18-month-old daughter, Hema, at the daycare near the station.

"He" from Hera, and "Ma" from Maria—a name that carries the grace of two mothers who help shape their love story.

There's no time to look for a window seat anymore. These days, Hanica only looks for two seats side by side. Every GO train ride is another quiet moment shared with Jake—a continuation of the ride that once sparks it all.

Hanica's parents visit often from Banff. Their voices fill the daily phone calls that connect the family across provinces. Jake and Hanica visit Jake's family every weekend. Hema's first word isn't "Mama" or "Dada"—it's "Ken." Her grandpa. Her favorite.

Aunt Mary and Jennie often join the weekends at Ken and Maria's home. Hema has started walking, and her tiny steps echo on the same garden path where Jake and Hanica walk as husband and wife.

Two photos hang on the entryway wall of Ken's home.

One: Jake and Hanica walking down the wedding aisle.

Two: The couple holding baby Hema in the same spot, love multiplied.

It all started on the GO train to Toronto Station.

But for Jake and Hanica, it had never just a transit stop.

The GO Station becomes their Love Station.

The place where they met as strangers, souls recognize each other, and a lifetime begins.

Now, love rides with them every day—in laughter, in shared coffee, in little fingers clutching theirs.

Their story continues—in gardens, train rides, and the soft miracle of love that only grows stronger with time.

www.ingramcontent.com/pod-product-compliance
Lightning Source LLC
Chambersburg PA
CBHW071205300726
48975CB00004B/1291